HAPPY FEET™

Friends Forever

By Siobhan Ciminera

A PRICE STERN SLOAN READER

PSS!
PRICE STERN SLOAN

Mumble and Gloria are
Emperor penguins.

They are also best friends!

Mumble and Gloria live in
Emperor Land with lots
of Emperor penguins.

Mumble and Gloria go
to Penguin Elementary.
At school, they learn
how to sing.

Every Emperor penguin
sings a Heartsong.
It is the voice all penguins
hear inside themselves.

Gloria has a beautiful song.

But Mumble can't sing at all!

The other penguins laugh

at him—but not Gloria.
She knows that it is not nice
to laugh at a friend.

Mumble and Gloria
are growing up.

And they are still
best friends!

Friends try new things together—
like swimming.

Friends do nice things for each other, like share a snack.

And friends are always
happy to see each other.

Gloria is the best singer
in Emperor Land.

The other penguins
love to hear her sing.

Mumble still can't sing.

But he is a great tap dancer.

Mumble wishes he could
sing like Gloria.

So he pretends to sing—
with a little help.

But Gloria likes Mumble
just the way he is.

Mumble shows Gloria
how to dance.
Now they can dance together!

Mumble must go far away
to find more fish.
Gloria will miss him.

She wishes she could come, too.
But sometimes friends have
to say good-bye.

Friends stay friends,
even when they are apart.
When Mumble comes back
to Emperor Land,

Gloria is so happy to see him!
Mumble is happy to see her, too.
That is because . . .

Mumble and Gloria will be
friends forever!